A Little Princess

By Frances Hodgson Burnett

Adapted by Cathy East Dubowski

A STEPPING STONE BOOK™
Random House New York

To my Little Princesses,
Lauren & Megan, with love
—C.E.D.

❦ ❦ ❦

Text copyright © 1994 by Random House, Inc. Cover illustration copyright © 2005 by Richard Jones. All rights reserved under International and Pan-American Copyright Conventions. Published in the United States by Random House Children's Books, a division of Random House, Inc., New York, and simultaneously in Canada by Random House of Canada Limited, Toronto. Originally published as a Bullseye Book by Random House, Inc., in 1994.

www.steppingstonesbooks.com/
www.randomhouse.com/kids

Library of Congress Cataloging-in-Publication Data
Dubowski, Cathy East.
A little princess / by Frances Hodgson Burnett ; adapted by Cathy East Dubowski; cover illustration by Richard Jones.
    p.   cm.
"A Stepping Stone book."
SUMMARY: Sara Crewe, a pupil at Miss Minchin's London school, is left in poverty when her father dies but is later rescued by a mysterious benefactor.
ISBN 0-679-85090-2 (pbk.) — ISBN 0-679-98011-3 (lib. bdg.)
[1. Boarding schools—Fiction. 2. Schools—Fiction. 3. Orphans—Fiction.
4. London (England)—History—1800–1950—Fiction. 5. Great Britain—History—Victoria, 1837–1901—Fiction.] I. Jones, Richard, ill. II. Burnett, Frances Hodgson, 1849–1924. Little princess. III. Title.
PZ7.D85445Li 2005   [E]—dc22   2004009255

Printed in the United States of America   26 25 24 23 22 21 20 19

Contents

1

Sara's New Home

"How odd things are," thought Sara Crewe.

She had been home not long ago. Home was Bombay, India, where the sun was bright and hot.

Then she and Papa got on a big ship. They sailed for days and days. The deck was steamy under the hot sun. The ocean seemed to go on forever.

Now they were in a strange new place. The crowded streets of London!

Sara looked out the carriage window. The sky was dark and gray. The fog was thick and damp. Gas lamps glowed in the windows of the shops. The day was as dark as night!

"Papa," she whispered. "Is this the place?"

Captain Crewe pulled his daughter close. "Yes, little Sara," he said softly. "We are here at last."

Sara was only seven. But she knew he was sad when he said it. "Well, Papa," she said. "We must make the best of it."

Captain Crewe laughed. Sara sounded so serious. Sometimes she seemed older than he was!

Captain Crewe was in the British army. The army had sent him to India, where Sara was born. So she was an English girl who had never been to England.

But Sara always knew she must leave India one day. India was much too hot for children. It was not good for their health. That's what the English mothers and fathers said.

The weather was milder in England. The children could go to good schools. They would learn to stand on their own two feet. Sooner or later every child was sent away.

And now it was Sara's turn.

Sara looked up at her young father. How handsome he was in his red uniform! Her mother had died when she was born. So he was all she had in the world.

Her father was rich. She had heard people say so. They said she would be rich one day too. But what did it mean to be rich? Sara didn't know.

They had many servants in India. Sara had an Indian ayah to look after her. She had books and clothes and toys.

But what good was all that? What good was it to be rich? She must still give up what she loved most. She must say goodbye to Papa.

The carriage clattered to a stop. Sara looked out. A row of brick houses stood before her. Each one looked the same. Tall and dull and ugly.

One house had a small brass sign. It

said: "Miss Minchin's School for Young Ladies."

"Here we are," said her father cheerfully. He twirled her down from the carriage. Then they climbed the steps and rang the bell.

A maid opened the door. She showed them into Miss Minchin's sitting room.

Sara looked around. The house had many nice things. Fine furniture. Thick rugs. Everything was polished and dusted.

But the house looked hard and unfriendly to Sara. It looked like a house just for show—not for living in.

"I don't like it," she whispered. "But even brave soldiers don't like going into battle. Do they, Papa?"

"Oh, Sara, my Little Soldier," he said. "What will I do without you?"

Then he hugged her hard and laughed. But Sara saw tears in his eyes.

At that moment Miss Minchin came in. She looked just like her house—tall, dull, and unfriendly. She had cold, fishy eyes and a cold, fishy smile.

"Captain Crewe," she said. "I am so pleased to have your daughter here." She looked down her nose at Sara. "Such a beautiful child!"

"Why does she say that?" Sara thought. "I am not beautiful. I don't have long golden hair or blue eyes. I have short black hair and green eyes. She is beginning by telling a lie."

Then Captain Crewe and Miss Minchin talked. He wanted Sara to have the best of everything. The prettiest bedroom. Her own sitting room. A French maid to replace her Indian ayah.

"I am sure Sara will do well in school," Captain Crewe said fondly. "She always has her nose in a book. She doesn't read them. She gobbles them up."

"How clever," Miss Minchin said with a stiff smile.

"Yes," said Captain Crewe. "But you

must make her play more. She should have lots of dolls."

"Oh, Papa," said Sara. "I wouldn't like lots of dolls. I couldn't be fond of them all. A doll should be special. Emily will be my special friend."

"Who is Emily?" Miss Minchin asked.

"She is a doll I haven't got yet," said Sara. "Papa is going to buy her for me. I have named her Emily. She will be my friend. Someone I can talk to when Papa is gone."

"Oh," said Miss Minchin, "what a darling child."

Sara thought her words sounded false. But Captain Crewe only smiled.

"Yes," he said, and held Sara close. "You must take good care of her for me."

2
Emily

Captain Crewe would leave England soon. So Sara spent every last minute with him.

Every day they went out to the shops. If Sara looked at something, her father bought it. He bought far more than Sara needed. Captain Crewe was young and spirited. He cared little for money. But he loved his daughter more than life itself. He wanted to give her everything.

They went to the fanciest dressmakers. They bought dresses in every color. Coats lined in fur. Hats trimmed with ostrich feathers. Gloves with tiny pearl buttons.

It was all much too grand for a girl of seven. But Captain Crewe did not see that. The shop girls whispered behind their hands. The child must be a princess from a faraway land!

Each day Sara looked for Emily. But she was not easy to find. "She must look real," Sara said. "As if she listens when I talk. Most dolls never seem to hear."

They looked at big dolls and small dolls. Dolls with black eyes and dolls with blue eyes. But none was Emily.

One day Sara and Captain Crewe took a walk. Suddenly Sara stopped.

"Papa!" she cried. "There's Emily!"

Captain Crewe looked into the window. A very pretty doll smiled out at them. Sara pulled him into the shop.

"Dear me," said Captain Crewe. "I feel as if someone should introduce us."

"You introduce me," said Sara. "And I will introduce you. But I knew her at once. So maybe she knows us, too."

Sara took the doll into her arms. She had golden-brown curls. Her eyes were blue. And she had real, soft eyelashes—not just lines painted on.

"Oh, yes," said Sara. "This is Emily."

So Emily was bought. Then it was back to the shops. For Emily must have new clothes too. Clothes as fine as Sara's.

The days in London were happy ones. But finally the time came for Captain Crewe to go home to India.

He gave Miss Minchin a card. It said: "Mr. Barrow and Mr. Skipworth."

"My lawyers," he said. "They handle all my business in England. You may send any bills to them. Remember: "Sara is to have *anything* she asks for."

Captain Crewe walked Sara to her room. It was time to say goodbye. Sara sat on her father's knee. She looked long and hard at his face.

"Are you learning me by heart, Little Soldier?"

"No, Papa," Sara whispered. "I know you by heart. You are *inside* my heart."

Then they hugged each other very tight. As if they would never let go.

3

French Lessons

The next morning Sara woke up. "Papa!" she thought. Then she remembered.

"He is at sea now," she told Emily. "We must be great friends."

Sara's maid, Mariette, came in. "Good morning!" she said in French. She helped Sara put on her school uniform. She tied pink ribbons in her hair.

Sara sat Emily in a tiny doll chair. Then she gave her a book. "Here," she said. "You may read while I am gone."

Mariette watched with wide eyes.

"I think dolls can do things," Sara explained. "Maybe Emily can read. Maybe she can walk and talk."

"Then why do we not see her?" asked Mariette.

"Oh, she won't do those things while we are here," said Sara. "What if people knew? They would put all the dolls to work. So the dolls keep it a secret."

Mariette laughed. "What funny ideas you have, my little one!"

Then it was time for school. Sara went downstairs. She could hear the girls laughing in the schoolroom.

Sara went in. Everyone hushed. Everyone stared.

But Sara did not mind. She wanted to know all about them, too.

Lavinia Herbert glared at the new girl. Lavinia was the oldest. She ruled the younger girls like a queen.

She poked her friend Jessie. "She is not even pretty," she whispered. "Her eyes are an odd color."

"But there is something interesting about her," said Jessie. "She makes you want to look at her again."

Lavinia frowned. She hated Sara already.

Miss Minchin came in and rapped on her desk. "Young ladies," she said. "This is your new friend, Miss Sara Crewe. She comes to us from far away. From India."

Sara smiled and made a curtsy.

"Sara," said Miss Minchin. "Your father hired a French maid for you. He must want you to study French."

"Excuse me," said Sara. "I think he hired her because he thought it would please me."

"My, my," Miss Minchin said. "Aren't we a spoiled little girl. Not everything is done just to please you! Believe me—your father wishes you to learn French."

But Sara knew how to speak French. She had always known how. Her mother had been French, and Papa spoke it often. Perhaps it helped him to remember her.

Sara was not sure what to say. "I—I have never really *learned* French, but—"

"That's enough," said Miss Minchin. "You have not learned it. You must begin at once. Here is your book. Monsieur

Dufarge will be here soon."

Sara sat down. She looked at the book. It was so simple and easy. She wanted to laugh. But Miss Minchin would not like that! So she tried to look serious.

Miss Minchin frowned. "You look very cross, Sara. I am sorry you do not want to learn French."

"I am very fond of it," said Sara. "But—"

"You must not always say 'but' when you are told to do things," said Miss Minchin. "Look at your book, please."

Sara did. She tried not to smile or frown.

Soon Monsieur Dufarge arrived. He smiled when he saw Sara. "Ah, a new student for me, Madame?"

"Yes," said Miss Minchin. "Her papa wants her to learn French. But I am afraid she is set against it."

"I am sorry of that," Monsieur Dufarge said. He smiled at Sara. "Maybe I can change your mind?"

Sara rose from her seat. Monsieur Dufarge had a kind face. Perhaps he would understand.

She began to explain. In French!

Miss Minchin's eyes nearly popped out of her head. Monsieur was delighted. "Ah! I cannot teach this child French!" he exclaimed. "Why, she *is* French!"

"Sara!" Miss Minchin grumbled. "You should have told me!"

"I—I tried," said Sara.

Lavinia and Jessie giggled behind their books. Miss Minchin's face turned red. Sara had made her look like a fool.

Then and there she began to dislike Sara Crewe.

Now Miss Minchin was very cross. Her eyes fell upon a fat little girl in the third row. She had long blond braids. And she was chewing on her ribbons.

"Miss St. John!" she cried. "Take those ribbons out of your mouth. Elbows off the desk! Sit up at once!"

The girl almost burst into tears.

Sara felt sorry for her. She watched her all morning. The girl had trouble with her lessons. Her French was very bad. Lavinia and the other girls laughed at her.

But Sara did not laugh. After lessons she sat down beside her. "My name is Sara," she said. "What's yours?"

The girl looked surprised. "Ermengarde," she said.

Sara said it slowly: "Er-men-garde. It's pretty, like a name in a fairy tale."

"Do you really think so?" Ermengarde said with a shy smile. Then she sighed. "You're so clever, Sara."

Ermengarde looked so sad. Sara had an idea. "Would you like to meet Emily?"

"Who is Emily?" asked Ermengarde.

"Come to my room and see," said Sara.

The two girls ran upstairs. Sara stopped at her door. "Shhh," she whispered. "Perhaps we will catch her!"

Sara listened. She looked through the keyhole. Then she threw open the door. The girls rushed inside.

But the room was quiet. Emily sat in her chair. The book was in her lap. She was just as Sara had left her.

"Oh!" said Sara. "She must have jumped into her seat."

"Can she really walk?" asked Ermengarde.

"I believe she can," said Sara. "At least, I pretend she can. That makes it seem true. Would you like to hold her?"

They sat on Sara's tiger skin rug. Sara told Ermengarde stories about India. But that made Sara think of her father. She sighed.

"Do you love your father?" Sara asked. "More than anything?"

Ermengarde didn't know how to answer. Her father was very smart. But he was ashamed of her. He could not stand that she was so stupid. Did she love her father? She did not know. She just tried to stay out of his way!

"I love mine more than all the world," said Sara. "But now he has gone away."

Ermengarde thought Sara might cry. But she didn't.

"I promised him I would be brave," Sara said. "Think how brave soldiers must be! Suppose there was a war. Papa would suffer. But he would never say a word. That's why I pretend. It helps you to bear things."

Ermengarde thought Sara was wonderful.

"Lavinia and Jessie are best friends," she said shyly. "Could *we* be best friends?" Then she blushed. Perhaps Sara would not want to be friends with a girl who was fat and stupid.

"Of course we can," Sara said with a smile. She squeezed Ermengarde's hand. "I'll even help you with French."

4
Friends and Enemies

Sunday morning dawned bright and clear. The girls put on their best dresses. They lined up two by two.

Lavinia took her place at the head of the line since she was the oldest. Her clothes were the latest style. She believed she deserved to be first. And she knew Miss Minchin liked to show her off.

At last Miss Minchin marched down the steps. Her fat, timid sister, Amelia, hurried after her. Lavinia smiled.

"Sara Crewe," Miss Minchin called. "Please come to the front of the line."

Lavinia's mouth flew open in surprise. So did Sara's. But Sara obeyed. She dragged Ermengarde with her.

Ermengarde giggled at Lavinia's scowl.

"Come, girls," Miss Minchin said. Then she stuck her long, thin nose in the air and marched them off to church.

Step by step, Lavinia's jealousy grew.

Sara soon made lots of friends.

The younger girls were used to being ordered about. Lavinia often made them cry.

But Sara never did. She took care of scraped knees. She helped with lessons, especially French. She gave tea parties in her room. She even let them play with Emily.

Most of the girls adored Sara.

Lavinia could hardly stand it. Miss Minchin was even worse, especially when parents came to visit.

"Sara dear," she would say. "Speak French for Lady Pitkin." Or, "Please tell the Wests about India."

Then Miss Minchin would smile. Sara was bright and rich. She had nice manners. She made the school look good. That made Miss Minchin look good too.

But she didn't really care about Sara. She cared about Captain Crewe's money!

What if Sara was not happy? Captain Crewe might take her out of school—and put his money somewhere else! So Miss Minchin treated Sara like a guest.

Sara might have been spoiled by all this. But she had too much sense.

"Things happen to people by accident," she told Ermengarde one day. "Good things and bad things. A lot of nice accidents happened to me. I just happen to have a rich father. I just happen to like books. Everyone has been kind to me. How could I not be nice?"

Sara shook her head. "Maybe I am really mean," she said. "But how will I ever know? What if nothing bad ever happens to me?"

"Lavinia has no troubles," said Ermengarde. "And look at her. She's horrid."

It was a very smart thought for a girl who was supposed to be so stupid.

5

Lottie

One day Sara heard screams. She ran to Miss Minchin's sitting room. But the door was closed.

"You bad child!" she heard Miss Minchin shout. Then the door flew open. Miss Minchin came out. Her glasses were crooked. Her hair was coming down. She looked as if she might bite!

Then she saw Sara. She cleared her throat and smoothed her hair. "Oh, Sara," she said.

Sara peeked in the door. Miss Amelia was wrestling with Lottie, the youngest girl in school. She lay on the floor, kicking and screaming.

"Perhaps I could help," said Sara. "May I try?"

"You are a clever child if you can!" Miss Minchin said sharply. Then she stopped herself. She must not be rude to Sara! She smiled her false, fishy smile. "But then, you are clever in everything, Sara. You are welcome to try." She and Miss Amelia were glad to leave.

Sara sat down beside Lottie. She didn't say a word. She just waited.

At first Lottie kept screaming. She often threw fits. Then grown-ups would pet her. Sometimes they would shout.

But Sara just sat there as if she didn't mind!

"I—haven't—got—a—mama!" Lottie wailed.

"Neither have I," said Sara.

Lottie stopped crying. This was new. "Where is she?"

"She went to heaven," said Sara. "But sometimes she watches over me. I'm sure your mama watches you, too. Perhaps they are both in this room right now."

Lottie looked around. What if her

mama was watching! She was not acting at all like the daughter of an angel!

Then Sara told Lottie about heaven. "There are fields of flowers where the angels play. The streets are pure gold. And no one ever gets tired."

"I want to go there!" Lottie cried. "I haven't got a mama at this school."

Sara took Lottie's hand. "I will be your mama," she said. "You will be my little girl. And Emily shall be your sister. Would you like that?"

Lottie smiled. "Oh, yes!" she said. Her tears were forgotten.

"Come, then," said Sara. "Let's wash your face. Then we'll brush your hair."

That was what had started all the fuss. But Lottie did not even remember.

She followed Mama Sara upstairs. Just like a good little angel.

6

Becky

It was a cold gray day. But Sara Crewe was warm and happy. She had on a fur-lined coat. Her pretty hat kept out the wind.

Sara stepped down from her carriage in front of the school. Then she looked around. She felt someone watching her.

Steps led to the basement kitchen. A face peeked out through the railing. A smudgy face with wide eyes.

Sara smiled. But the face disappeared.

That night Sara sat before the fire, telling a story. The girls crowded into her room. They loved Sara's stories. She didn't just tell them. She became part of them. She made them seem real.

A servant girl slipped into the room.

The one with the smudgy face! She carried a heavy coal box. She added coal to the fire. She kept her head down. But Sara could tell she was listening.

The little maid swept the hearth. Very, very slowly.

Suddenly she dropped her cleaning brush. It clattered on the hearth.

"That girl has been listening!" Lavinia cried.

The maid ran from the room.

"I knew she was listening," Sara said angrily. "Why shouldn't she?"

"I don't know about *your* mama," said Lavinia. "But mine wouldn't like it. Telling stories to servant girls!"

"My mama wouldn't care," said Sara. "She knows that stories belong to everyone."

"I thought your mama was dead," said Lavinia meanly. Then she laughed and dragged Jessie out the door.

Later that night Mariette came in. She helped Sara undress for bed.

"Who is that new servant girl?" asked Sara. "The one who makes the fires?"

"Her name is Becky," said Mariette. "She is the new kitchen maid. Poor girl. They make her do everything. Wash windows. Scrub floors. Clean the girls' boots. Everyone shouts, 'Becky, do this! Becky, do that!'"

Mariette tucked Sara into bed and said good night. But Sara could not sleep. She could not stop thinking about Becky. She hoped she would see her again.

A few weeks later she did.

Sara had been to dancing class. She had on a pink dress. She had roses pinned in her dark hair. She twirled into her room—and stopped.

There sat Becky, the little kitchen maid. She had fallen asleep before the fire. There were coal smudges on her tired face. Her cap had fallen sideways.

Then the fire popped. Becky jumped awake. "Oh, miss!" she cried. "I'm ever so sorry."

Sara laughed gently. "You couldn't help it."

"Ain't you mad?" Becky asked. "Ain't you going to tell Miss Minchin?"

"Of course not," said Sara.

Becky still looked frightened. So Sara sat down beside her. "Don't be afraid, Becky. We are the same, you and I. I am only a little girl. Just like you."

Becky didn't know about that! But she smiled a little.

"Would you like some cake?" asked Sara.

Becky could hardly believe it. She was sitting before a warm fire. She was talking with a young lady. And the young lady had offered her cake! She must be dreaming. But she gladly took the cake.

"Once I seen a real princess," said Becky shyly. "She was dressed all in pink. She looked just like you!"

"How lovely to be a princess," said Sara. "I wonder what it feels like." She sat up straight in her chair. "I know. I shall begin to pretend I am one."

Sara smiled to herself. What might a princess do for Becky?

"Did you like my stories?" she asked.

"Oh, yes, miss," said Becky.

"Then try to do my room at the same time each day," said Sara. "I'll be here and tell you part of a story."

"Oh, miss!" said Becky. "I wouldn't care how heavy the coal box is. Or what the cook does to me. Not if I had your story to think on each day."

Soon Becky hurried back to work. She had an extra piece of cake in her pocket. And a smile on her smudgy face.

7

Diamond Mines

India was too far from London for Captain Crewe to visit Sara. But he wrote to her often.

One day Sara got a letter. She ran to her room to read it. "Oh, Emily," she said. "It's good news."

Her father had met an old school friend. The man owned land where diamonds had been found. He was going to hire workers to build mines and dig for diamonds.

It was such a sure thing. Captain Crewe gave most of his money to his friend. Now they were partners.

"We shall be rich beyond our wildest dreams," wrote Captain Crewe. "What do you think of that, Little Soldier?"

The girls could talk of nothing else.

"What a silly story," Lavinia muttered.

"I think you hate Sara," said Jessie.

"No, I don't," said Lavinia. "I just don't believe in mines full of diamonds. Sara is making it all up."

"Do you know what I heard?" Jessie whispered. "Sara likes to pretend she is a princess. She plays it all the time. Even in school."

"Really?" said Lavinia. She smiled thoughtfully.

That afternoon Sara came into the schoolroom. Lavinia was teasing Lottie. Lottie was crying.

Sara ran to stand between them. "Stop it, Lavinia!"

"Oh, forgive me, Your Royal Highness," said Lavinia. She bowed low. "I suppose I must obey. You are a princess. Isn't that right? Princess Sara? Our school will be all the fashion now."

Sara's face burned. Her pretending was

special. How awful to hear Lavinia make fun of it—in front of the whole school!

Sara felt like shouting. She felt like pulling Lavinia's hair.

But—princesses did *not* fly into rages.

"It's true," Sara said. "Sometimes I do pretend I'm a princess. And I always try to act like one."

Lavinia had tried to make Sara look bad in front of the young ladies.

But the young ladies loved stories about princesses. They stared at Sara as if she were a real princess!

Now everyone called her Princess Sara.

Lavinia and Jessie said it to make fun of her.

But most girls said it with love. In their eyes Sara was truly a princess.

8

A Perfect Party

Sara's birthday was coming. Her father wrote that he was planning for her party—even though he could not come.

He had written Miss Minchin, too, he said. He had told her to order all kinds of presents. Even a new doll from Paris. Would that be a good present?

Sara sighed. Papa was so far away. He could not see her growing up. She no longer played with dolls much. There was Emily, of course. But that was different.

She wrote back: "I am getting very old, Papa. This will be my last doll. No one could take Emily's place. But I shall respect the Last Doll very much."

Far away in India, Captain Crewe sat

in his study. He was ill with fever. His desk was piled high with bills. He was not very good at business. And he was worried about the diamond mines....

Then he opened Sara's letter. He read it through. And he laughed as he had not laughed in weeks.

"What fun she is!" he said. "How I wish she were with me right now!"

Sara woke up. It was her birthday at last. She ran into her sitting room. A small present lay on the table.

Sara tore it open. It was a red flannel pincushion. Black pins spelled out: "Menny hapy reterns."

The flannel was old and dirty. The spelling was not quite right. But Sara was delighted. She knew it was from Becky.

Just then Becky peeped in the door. "Do you like it, Miss Sara?" she asked.

"I love it!" Sara replied.

Becky grinned. "I sat up nights and made it. I knew you could pretend it was satin with diamond pins."

Sara hugged her friend. "Oh, Becky. I do love you."

"Thank you, miss," said Becky shyly. "But, golly! It ain't worth all that. The flannel ain't even new."

At last it was time for the party. Sara wore a new silk dress. Mariette put flowers in her hair.

Sara was so excited! She wanted to run downstairs. But Miss Minchin said no. They marched into the schoolroom, like a royal parade. First Sara. Next Miss Minchin. Then the servants with all her presents. Becky tagged along at the end.

"Silence, young ladies," Miss Minchin said. Then she noticed Becky.

"Becky!" she cried. "It is not your place to look at the young ladies. Leave at once."

"Please, Miss Minchin," said Sara. "May Becky stay to see the presents?"

Miss Minchin did not like this idea one bit. But she must keep rich little Sara happy.

"Oh, very well, Sara," said Miss Minchin. "But only because it's your birthday. Becky! Stand over there. Not too near my young ladies."

Becky smiled with delight. She didn't care where she stood. As long as she could stay!

Miss Minchin cleared her throat. "Now. Sara's birthdays are very important. When she is grown—"

"Excuse me, sister," Miss Amelia interrupted. "Captain Crewe's lawyer, Mr. Barrow, is here to see you."

"Oh," said Miss Minchin. "Well. Enjoy your party, young ladies."

As soon as Miss Minchin left, the "young ladies" sprang from their chairs. "Open your presents, Sara!" they cried.

Sara opened the first box. The girls groaned. "Books!"

"Your father is as bad as mine," said Ermengarde.

Sara laughed. "I like them."

Then she reached for the biggest box.

Slowly she opened it. The girls pressed closer around her.

It was the Last Doll. The one her father had ordered. She was beautiful!

"She is almost as big as Lottie!" one girl gasped.

Sara opened the doll's trunk. One by one she lifted out her things. There were ball dresses and tea gowns. Hats and fans. A necklace and a crown that looked as if they were real diamonds!

Even Lavinia and Jessie pushed to see. They forgot they were too old for dolls!

Sara tried a black velvet hat on the doll. "Suppose she understands us," she said with a gleam in her eye. "Suppose she likes being admired."

"Oh, Sara," Lavinia said crossly. "You are always supposing things."

"I know," said Sara. "It's fun."

"But it's easy for you," Lavinia said. "You have everything. What if you were poor?"

Sara looked thoughtful. "Perhaps I

would have to suppose *all* the time," she replied. "But it might not be so easy."

Just then Miss Amelia came in. "Come along, girls," she said. "The birthday cake is ready."

"Cake!" the girls squealed. Laughing, they tugged Princess Sara to her feast.

At last the room was quiet. Everyone was gone. Everyone but Becky. She crept out from the corner. She'd never seen such presents. She just had to have one more look!

She touched the Last Doll's hair. She picked up the glittering crown. "Blimey..." she whispered.

Suddenly she heard someone coming. What if they thought Becky was stealing!

Becky ducked beneath the table. She pulled the tablecloth down just as the doorknob turned.

9

Terrible News

Becky trembled beneath the table as the door opened.

Miss Minchin came in with Mr. Barrow. "Please be seated," she said.

But the lawyer did not sit. He frowned at the Last Doll. "What a waste of money!" he said.

"Captain Crewe is a rich man," Miss Minchin said smugly. "Why, his diamond mines—"

"There are no diamond mines."

Miss Minchin blinked. "I beg your pardon?"

"Yes," said Mr. Barrow. "The late Captain Crewe—"

"The *late* Captain Crewe! What do

you mean?" Miss Minchin demanded.

"He's dead," Mr. Barrow said flatly. "He died of jungle fever. So they say. But I think his money troubles were the death of him."

Miss Minchin's hands began to tremble. "What money troubles?" she whispered.

"Captain Crewe was very foolish," said Mr. Barrow. "He put all his money into his friend's mines. But they never found any diamonds. His friend ran away.

"Captain Crewe was sick when the news came. The shock was too great for him. He died, calling for his little girl. And he didn't leave her a single penny."

Miss Minchin stumbled into a chair. "Wh-what are you saying?" she said. "That Sara will have no fortune?"

"None," said Mr. Barrow. "And she hasn't a relative in the world. I am afraid she is your problem now."

Miss Minchin's cold, fishy mouth hung open. She stared into space. It just couldn't be true!

Suddenly girlish laughter broke into her thoughts. She remembered the party. The party with all the food. And all those expensive presents!

Miss Minchin had paid for them out of her own pocket. She had put them on Captain Crewe's bill. Now that bill would never be paid!

"I have been robbed!" she cried. "I shall turn her out into the streets!"

Mr. Barrow went to the door. "I wouldn't do that if I were you," he said. "It would make your school look bad. Think what people will say: 'Miss Minchin turned a poor orphan out into the streets.'"

"But what can I do?" Miss Minchin cried.

"Keep her and make use of her," said Mr. Barrow. "Make her work off the bills."

Mr. Barrow opened the door and bumped into Miss Amelia. She had been trying to listen at the keyhole! "Good day!" he said, and stalked off with a frown.

"Amelia," Miss Minchin said. Her

voice sounded odd, as if someone were squeezing her throat. "Does Sara have a plain black dress?"

"Yes, an old velvet one," said Miss Amelia. "But it is worn and way too small for her. I don't think—"

"Amelia!" Miss Minchin glared at her sister. "Tell Sara to take off that silly party dress. Tell her to put on the black one. Then bring her to me."

"What in the world has happened?" asked Miss Amelia. She was trembling now. She was always afraid of her sister. But she had never seen her look like this. She looked like a teakettle about to boil over!

"Captain Crewe is dead," said Miss Minchin. "And he didn't leave Sara a penny."

"Oh, no!" said Miss Amelia.

"Don't stand there like a goose!" snapped Miss Minchin. "Go tell her."

"But why should I—"

"Now!"

Miss Amelia scurried out like a mouse.

Miss Minchin glared at the presents on the table. "Princess Sara indeed!"

Then she heard a sob. It came from under the table.

"Who's there?" she cried. "Come out this instant!"

Becky crawled out, sobbing.

"How dare you!" said Miss Minchin.

"Oh, please, mum," Becky prattled through her tears. "What will Miss Sara do now? May I wait on her now that she's poor?"

"No!" she cried. "She will wait on herself—and other people as well. Now leave or I'll toss you into the streets too."

Becky threw her apron over her head. She ran out in tears. "It's just like in them stories," she wailed. "The ones where the princesses are thrown out into the cold."

10
How Things Changed

Sara came to Miss Minchin's sitting room. She wore her old black dress. It was way too short and far too tight. But Sara walked as if she were wearing her finest silk dress.

Her eyes were ringed with dark shadows. But she had not been crying. She held Emily tightly in her arms.

"Put down that doll!" said Miss Minchin. "What do you mean by bringing her here?"

"No," said Sara quietly. "I will not put her down. Papa gave her to me."

"Well! You have no time for dolls now!" Miss Minchin said with a snort. "Did Miss Amelia explain things?"

"Yes," said Sara. "My papa...My papa is dead."

"You are a beggar," said Miss Minchin cruelly. "You have no relatives. No home. No one to take care of you."

Sara's face twitched slightly. But she said nothing.

"Are you stupid?" Miss Minchin demanded. "Can you not understand? You are all alone in the world. You have *nothing* unless I give you a home."

"I understand," said Sara quietly.

"Your party. That silly doll with all her fancy clothes. *I* paid the bills!" Miss Minchin cried.

Sara looked away. "The Last Doll..."

"The Last Doll indeed!" said Miss Minchin. "That doll is mine, not yours! Everything you own is now mine."

"Then please take it away," said Sara.

Miss Minchin had thought Sara would be frightened. She had thought Sara would cry. But the child just stood there, silent and proud. Like a princess!

"Don't put on grand airs with me," Miss Minchin snapped. "You are not a 'princess' anymore. You are like Becky now. You must work for your living."

A sparkle came into Sara's eyes. "Oh, may I work?" she said. "Then it will not matter so much. What can I do?"

Miss Minchin could not believe her ears. How could the child sound happy about that! "You will do whatever you are told!" she said. "Now go!"

Sara turned to leave.

"Stop!" cried Miss Minchin. "Aren't you going to thank me?"

Sara looked back, surprised. "For what?" she asked.

"For my kindness to you," said Miss Minchin. "For giving you a home."

Sara shook her head. "No, Miss Minchin. You are *not* kind. And this is *not* a home."

Then Sara ran from the room.

Slowly she climbed the stairs. She hugged Emily tight. She wanted to go lie down on the tiger skin. She wanted to look into the fire and think and think.

At last she reached her room. She put her hand to the doorknob. But then Miss Amelia came out, looking embarrassed. She closed the door behind her.

"I'm sorry. You can't go in there," she said. Her face turned red. "It's not your room anymore."

Sara tried to keep her voice from shaking. "Where is my room?" she asked.

Miss Amelia twisted her hands. She looked away. "Your room is next to Becky's," she mumbled. "It's in the attic."

Sara turned and climbed the steps. The stairway grew narrow and dark. Finally she reached the room in the attic. She opened the door. And her heart sank.

The room was small and gray. The roof was slanted. There was a skylight. But it framed a patch of dull gray sky.

An old iron bed stood in one corner. The blanket was worn, and the pillow was small and dirty. The floor was bare.

Sara sat down on an old stool. She put her head in her arms. But still she did not cry.

A soft tap at the door made her look up. Becky came in. Her eyes were red from crying.

Sara tried to smile, but she couldn't. She held out her hand.

"Oh, Becky!" she said. "I told you we were just the same. Just two little girls. See how true it is? I am not a princess anymore."

Becky knelt and took Sara's hand. "Oh, yes you are, miss," she said. "You'll always be a princess. Nothing can ever change that."

II

The Attic

Sara would never forget her first night in the attic. Her bed was hard. The room was cold and dark. The wind howled around the chimney tops.

But that was not all. Sara heard sounds behind the walls. Scratchy, squeaky sounds. She knew what that meant. Rats!

Tiny claws skittered across the floor. Sara jerked the thin blanket over her head. At last she fell asleep, whispering in the dark. "Papa is dead. Papa is dead...."

When she woke up the next morning, she was cold. She did not know where she was at first. "Papa!" she thought. Then she remembered.

Sara jumped out of bed, shivering. The floor was ice cold. Quickly she dressed and ran downstairs. The door to her old room was open. But all her things were gone.

"When did Mariette leave?" Sara wondered. "She didn't even say goodbye."

Sara went down to breakfast. She used to sit next to Miss Minchin. Now Lavinia sat there, grinning like a cat.

"Sara," Miss Minchin said sharply. "You must begin your duties. Sit with the young girls. Keep them quiet. Where were you? Lottie has already upset her tea."

So began Sara's new life. She was the first one up and the last to go to sleep. The cook and housemaids ordered her about. Sara was blamed if anything went wrong!

Sara worked hard. She would show them. She wanted to work for her living. She did not want charity.

But weeks went by. No one ever told her what a good worker she was. They just gave her more to do!

Sara was no longer allowed to go to school. But sometimes she went to the schoolroom late at night.

"I'm so tired," she told Emily. "But I must not forget what I have learned."

The young ladies did not know what to think. Sara was so different now. Her dress was shabby. She ran through the dirty streets on errands for the cook!

Even worse, Sara no longer laughed or told them stories.

Sara had once seemed like a princess. Now she was just a servant. Miss Minchin would not let them play with her.

Slowly they began to forget why they had loved her.

This hurt Sara more than anything. But she didn't show it. "Soldiers don't complain," she told Emily.

At least, she had Becky. They were too busy to talk during the day. But sometimes at night they tapped secret messages on the wall between their rooms.

One day Sara was going down the stairs with a basket of laundry.

Ermengarde was coming up.

Sara looked so different! Poor Ermengarde could not think what to say.

"How—how are you?" Ermengarde stammered. "Are you—unhappy?"

Sara was tired and cross. And she thought, "Ermengarde is like the others. She does not really want to talk to me."

Sara's feelings were hurt. So her words were harsh.

"What do you think!" she snapped. "Do you think I am happy?" Then she hurried down the stairs with her heavy basket.

A few days later Sara had more work than ever. It was late when she crept up the stairs. A light shone beneath her door. Someone was in there!

Slowly Sara opened the door.

"Ermengarde! Why are you here?" said Sara. "You will get into trouble."

"I don't care!" cried Ermengarde. "Oh, Sara. Why don't you like me anymore?"

"What!" said Sara. "I *do* like you. But everything is different now. I thought you were different too."

"*You* are the one who is different," said Ermengarde. "You won't talk to me. I didn't know what to do."

Sara saw that she had been wrong. She threw her arms around Ermengarde. They laughed with tears in their eyes.

Then Ermengarde looked around. "Oh, Sara, can you bear to live here?"

"I suppose I must," said Sara. "Perhaps I can pretend it's different."

Sara had almost forgotten about pretending. Now her eyes began to shine.

"I am a prisoner in the Bastille," she announced. "Miss Minchin is the jailer. Becky is the prisoner in the next cell!"

"Oh, Sara," whispered Ermengarde. "It's like a story!"

"It *is* a story," said Sara. "I'm a story. You're a story. Even Miss Minchin is a story. *Everything* is a story."

Ermengarde was so happy. Sara looked like herself again.

And they were friends once more.

12
Two Visitors

Lottie heard the gossip about Sara. But she did not really understand. Sara still helped the younger girls with French. Yet something was different.

"Are you very poor now, Sara?" Lottie asked one day during French. "Are you as poor as a beggar?"

"Beggars have no place to live," said Sara. "I do."

"Where?" said Lottie. "Is it nice? Can I come see?"

"Hush," said Sara. "Miss Minchin is looking."

One day Lottie heard the older girls talking. Sara was in the attic! Lottie climbed the stairs to Sara's room. She pushed open the door.

"Mama Sara!" Lottie cried. She looked around. Then she burst into tears.

"Don't cry, Lottie," said Sara. "It's not so bad."

Lottie stopped crying. "*Why* isn't it so bad?" she asked.

Sara took her hand. She showed her the skylight. "You can see all sorts of things from here," she said. "Things you can't see downstairs. You can see sparrows talking to each other. You can see chimney smoke making wreaths in the sky. It's like another world."

"I want to see!" said Lottie.

Sara lifted Lottie to the window. The sparrows came when Sara called. Lottie took a bun from her pocket. Sara was so hungry. She could have eaten it in three bites. But Lottie fed it to the birds.

The attic next door had a window, but the house was empty. "Suppose a girl lived there," said Sara. "We could talk to each other across the rooftops."

Then Sara walked Lottie around the bare little room. "Suppose my room had a blue rug. A sofa just there. Imagine bookshelves. A lamp with a rose-colored shade. A table set for tea."

Sara made everything seem so real. Lottie could almost see it all. "I like this attic, Mama Sara," she said. "I want to live here too."

Lottie was happy now. But she could go back downstairs whenever she wanted. She could go back to her warm, pretty room. Sara had to stay in the attic.

"Goodbye, Mama Sara," Lottie said at last. "I'll visit you again soon."

Sara watched her go. She closed her door. The pretend things faded away.

Then something moved—there, in the shadows!

A large rat sat on his hind legs. He sniffed the air. He looked so funny—like a little man with whiskers! Sara was not afraid.

Sara imagined the rat had a family. His children were hungry and crying. So Papa Rat was hunting for food.

Sara held out a few crumbs from Lottie's bread. She sat very still. Papa Rat seemed not to fear her. He crept forward. He snatched the crumbs. Then he ran back into the wall.

13
The Large Family

Ermengarde and Lottie could not come to visit often. It was dangerous. Miss Minchin might catch them.

So Sara lived a strange lonely life.

Once she had gone about in a carriage. She had worn beautiful clothes. People had stopped and smiled at her. But no one smiled at a shabby servant girl. No one even looked at her.

Sara was lonely, even in the crowded streets of London. So she made up stories about the people she saw.

There was one house not far from Miss Minchin's. It was Sara's favorite. The family that lived there had eight children! Sara called them the Large Family.

She often saw the children. Sometimes they took walks with their nanny. Sometimes they went out in the carriage with their mother.

At night she often saw them greet their father. They always surrounded him and poked in his pockets for presents. Most of the time they found something!

The Large Family always seemed so happy. Sara grew quite fond of them.

One evening she was walking past the Large Family's house. Suddenly the door flew open. The children ran down the steps, laughing and shouting.

The girls stepped up into the carriage. But the boy stared at Sara. He seemed to be about five. Sara smiled at him.

The boy looked Sara up and down. He had heard stories about poor children. Here was a real one! He reached into his pocket and pulled out a coin.

"Here, little girl," he said.

Sara's face turned red. The boy thought she was a beggar! Like the ragged children she had once given money to. Did she really look so bad?

"No, thank you," Sara said politely.

But the boy would not give up. He thrust the small coin into her hand.

"You must take it, poor little girl!" he said. "Buy food with it."

He was trying so hard to be kind. Sara couldn't say no. It would be cruel to be so proud.

So she took the coin. "Thank you," she said with a curtsy. "You are a kind, darling little thing."

The boy grinned proudly and got in the carriage. But now his sisters stared. That girl! She seemed so poor—but she spoke so well. And she had the manners of a princess. She couldn't be a beggar. Who could she be?

14
Neighbors from India

One day Sara saw something wonderful. Someone was moving in next door. Maybe she'd see a face at the attic window soon. Someone she could talk to!

Sara stopped to watch the movers. The new neighbors had fine furniture. A carved teakwood table. A beautiful screen. A statue of an Indian god.

Why, her father had had a statue just like that back home. Someone in this family must have been to India!

Suddenly Sara felt homesick. Her heart ached as she closed her eyes and remembered India.

She could feel the hot sun and see the bright colors. She could hear her sweet, gentle ayah singing an Indian song. She could see her handsome father laughing.

Sara opened her eyes and smiled. She felt sad—but happy, too. The neighbors' Indian treasures had helped make her memories sharp and clear.

It was as if they had brought her a tiny piece of home.

A few weeks later Sara was cleaning windows. She looked out. A carriage stopped at the curb. The father of the Large Family helped a man step down.

"My new neighbor," thought Sara. The man was very thin. He struggled to climb the steps to his door. Soon after, the doctor came.

"He must be very ill," thought Sara. "Perhaps kind thoughts can reach people, even through windows and doors."

She closed her eyes. She tried to send him her thoughts: "Get well soon."

That night Sara stood at her window. There was one good thing about the attic room. The beautiful sunsets! Sara felt she had the whole world to herself.

Then she heard an odd sound. She looked next door.

A man stood at the attic window. His clothes were all white. His head was wrapped in a turban. He was an Indian manservant! He held a chattering monkey in his arms. His eyes looked sad as he watched the sunset.

"Perhaps he is homesick for India too," Sara thought.

Suddenly the monkey sprang from the man's arms. He dashed across the roof and jumped in through Sara's window. She laughed as he ran around the room.

Sara called to the man, "Will he let me catch him?"

The man was surprised. Sara had spoken to him in his own Indian language!

He answered in the same language. "He is a good monkey. He will not bite. But he is hard to catch. My name is Ram Dass. May I come get him?"

"Can you get across?" she asked.

"Just watch," he said. Ram Dass crossed easily. He moved as if he had walked on rooftops all his life. He dropped to Sara's floor without a sound.

The monkey ran from him, but it was all in play. At last Ram Dass caught him, and the monkey clung to his neck. Sara could tell the man was kind.

Ram Dass was shocked by Sara's room. But he said nothing. He acted as if he were in a fancy sitting room.

"The monkey belongs to my master, Mr. Carrisford," he said. "He is very ill, but the monkey makes him laugh. He would be sad if the monkey were lost. Thank you for your help."

Ram Dass bowed to Sara. Then he carried the monkey home.

Sara thought of many things that night.

She longed to run away, just like the monkey. To India. To the life she had once had, when she was happy and free.

But that life was gone forever. It could

have been a dream. It could have been a story she made up.

For a long time Sara lay awake in the dark. What did the future hold for her? Another day, another year as a dirty, hungry servant?

It seemed so hopeless. And yet, something would not let her give up.

"It would be easy to be a princess in gowns of gold," Sara told herself. "But I can still be a princess inside—even though I am dressed in rags."

Sara went to sleep then, and her dreams were peaceful.

15

On the Other Side of the Wall

Sara did her work cheerfully the next day. Once Miss Minchin scolded her in front of the young ladies. Sara only smiled.

But Miss Minchin was in a very bad mood. Sara's smile seemed rude. So she slapped Sara Crewe across the face!

Sara was stunned. The young ladies gasped. Even Miss Minchin seemed surprised.

Sara stood still a moment. Then she could not help herself.

She laughed.

"What are you laughing at?" Miss Minchin cried.

"I was thinking," said Sara.

"How dare you think," said Miss

Minchin. "What were you thinking?"

"I was thinking how surprised you would be," said Sara. "How frightened. If you suddenly found out—"

"Found out what?" Miss Minchin asked nervously.

"That I was a real princess."

The young ladies stared. Miss Minchin's fishy mouth hung open.

"Go to your room this instant!" shouted Miss Minchin.

Sara made a little curtsy. Just like a real princess. Then she left the room.

The girls began to chatter.

"Young ladies!" Miss Minchin shouted. "Attend to your lessons!"

Next door Thomas Carrisford stared into the fire.

"I must find her," he said. "She may be alone and penniless. She may be begging in the street."

"Do not worry," said the father of the Large Family. His name was Mr. Carmichael. He was Thomas Carrisford's lawyer. "We will find her. And then you can give her her fortune."

Carrisford shook his head. The memories haunted him.

The diamond mines had held such promise! Then they seemed to fail. He thought he'd lost all his money.

Still, he could live with that. But what of his friend Captain Crewe? He had thought he had lost his money too.

But as it turned out, the mines were not worthless. They were *filled* with diamonds.

"My friend trusted me," said Mr. Carrisford. "But he died thinking I had ruined him! How he must have hated me!"

"You must not blame yourself," said Mr. Carmichael. "You were ill when all this happened. You were not yourself."

Carrisford dropped his head in his hands. He knew Captain Crewe had a daughter. He knew she had gone away to school. If only he could remember where!

"Sometimes I dream of him," said Carrisford. "He always asks the same question. 'Tom! Where is my Little Soldier?'"

He grabbed Mr. Carmichael's hand. "I must answer him!" he cried. "You must help me find her."

Night came to the square. One by one the lights winked out. But two people were still awake long after the square was quiet.

One was Thomas Carrisford. He sat in his study, staring into the fire.

The other was Sara Crewe. She curled up on her hard bed. She stared up at the sky.

"Oh, Papa," she whispered. "It seems so long ago since you were here. Since I was your Little Soldier."

Sara had no way of knowing her father's friend was looking for her. That he was just on the other side of the wall.

And Mr. Carrisford did not know the girl he was looking for was right next door.

16

The Hungry Child

It was an icy winter day. Sara clutched her market basket. She held her tattered hat against the wind. Her feet were freezing in the slushy streets. And she'd had nothing to eat all day.

The wind picked up. Sara put her head down.

Then she saw something. There! Something glittered in the gutter. She leaned down and picked it up.

A silver fourpenny piece!

Sara had just passed a shop. Mrs. Brown's Bakery. Now she looked inside. A woman put a tray of hot buns in the window. Sara's stomach growled.

Sara started to go in. But a child sat on the steps. Her face was dirty. Her hair was tangled. She was a bundle of rags! She stared at Sara with empty eyes.

"Are you hungry?" Sara asked the girl. "When did you last eat?"

"Dunno," the girl whispered.

"Wait here," Sara said.

She went into the bakery shop. "Excuse me," she said. "Have you lost a silver fourpence?"

Mrs. Brown looked up. She stared at Sara's thin face and ragged clothes. Clothes that had once been fine.

"Bless us, no," she said. "Did you find one?"

"Yes," said Sara. "In the gutter."

"Keep it, then," said Mrs. Brown. "Goodness knows who lost it. You could never find out."

Sara smiled with relief. "Four buns, then, please," she said. "Those that are a penny each."

Mrs. Brown went to the window. She put four buns in a bag. She glanced at Sara. Then she dropped in two more.

"I said four, if you please," said Sara. "I only have fourpence."

"Ah, well," said Mrs. Brown. "I can't put them back now, can I?"

She smiled at Sara. Then several people came in. She went to wait on them.

Sara went back outside. The girl was still there.

"Here," said Sara. She held out a bun.

The child stared at her. Then she snatched the bread. She tore at it like a wild animal.

Sara sighed and gave her three more buns. She had never seen anyone so hungry!

Sara watched the girl eat. She put her hand in the bag one more time. She pulled out the fifth bun. Her hand trembled. Then she put the bun on the girl's lap.

The girl was too hungry even to say thank you.

"Goodbye," Sara said. Then she disappeared into the crowd.

Mrs. Brown saw it all. She opened the

door. "How many buns did that girl give you?" she asked the child.

"Five."

"She kept only one for herself?" Mrs. Brown exclaimed. She shook her head. "I'm sure she could have eaten all six." She looked at the ragged girl again.

"Are you still hungry?" she asked.

"I'm always hungry," said the girl.

Mrs. Brown held open the door. "Then come inside."

Sara walked home with her bun. She tore off tiny pieces and ate slowly. It would last longer that way.

It was dark now. The lights were on in all the houses. Sara could see in the windows. She saw the gentleman next door. He was staring into the fire.

Across the square a door opened. The Large Family came out. The children kissed their father goodbye.

"We hope you find the little girl!" called the boy.

Mr. Carmichael got into his carriage. He was off to Paris, and then to Russia. He was off to search for a little girl. The lost daughter of Captain Crewe.

Sara watched the father of the Large Family drive away. Slowly she ate the last bite of bun. It was all the supper she'd get that night.

17

The Secret Party

Papa Rat crawled out of the wall. He sniffed the air. Sara was gone. But something was happening in the attic.

The window opened. Two men dropped to the floor. One was Ram Dass. The other was Mr. Carrisford's secretary.

Papa Rat ran back into the wall.

"Was that a rat?" the young man cried.

"Yes," said Ram Dass. "There are many in the walls."

"Ugh," said the man. "How can the child stand it?"

Ram Dass smiled. "The child is the friend of all things. I see her when she does not see me. The sparrows come when she calls. She has tamed the rat."

The secretary took out a notebook.

"What a place!" he said. He walked around the room. He wrote down notes.

Ram Dass smiled. He had shared an idea with Mr. Carrisford. Now they were going to make it come true.

Soon the two men left.

Papa Rat felt it was safe to come out again. Perhaps they had left some crumbs.

Cook had sent Sara to the market. But Sara still had many things to get. She hurried from shop to shop. She slipped in the mud and fell down. People turned and stared at her. Some even laughed.

Sara walked home in the dark. She was muddy and late. And she still did not have everything on her list.

"Why didn't you stay all night?" Cook snapped as she took the market basket. "Where are the rest of my things?"

"The shops closed before I could get it all," said Sara. "I'm sorry."

"Why, you worthless girl!" cried Cook.

"Please," said Sara. "May I have my dinner?"

"What!" cried Cook. "Does Princess Sara expect a hot supper? Not this late, my girl. Not even for a princess. Especially one who doesn't do her work. There's some bread. That's all you'll get tonight!"

The bread was hard and dry. But Sara took it. Yawning, she went to her room.

Ermengarde was waiting for her. She sat on the bed, wrapped in a red shawl. "Look, Sara. Papa sent me more books."

Sara's troubles were forgotten. She picked up a book. Carefully she turned the pages. "How beautiful!" she whispered.

"Papa will ask me questions about them," Ermengarde said. "What shall I do?"

"I'll read them," said Sara. "Then I will tell you all the stories."

"Oh, would you, Sara?" said Ermengarde. "Papa will be happy if I learn anything."

Suddenly they heard footsteps on the stairs. Sara put her finger to her lips. She blew out the candle.

Miss Minchin was shouting at Becky.

"You greedy little thief!" cried Miss Minchin. "A whole meat pie is missing. You should be sent to prison!"

"It weren't me, mum," Becky sobbed. "I swear!"

"Liar!" cried Miss Minchin. "Go to bed this instant." Sara and Ermengarde heard Miss Minchin slap Becky's face! Then they heard her stomp downstairs.

"That wicked woman!" Sara whispered. She lit the candle again. Her face looked hard.

"Cook steals food," she continued. "I've seen her! She gives it to her policeman boyfriend. Becky is hungry. But she never steals. Sometimes she eats scraps from the trash."

Then Ermengarde saw something strange. Something she had never seen before. She saw Sara cry.

"Sara," Ermengarde said. "Are *you* ever hungry?"

Sara was so tired. So hungry. So angry at Miss Minchin for being mean to Becky.

"Yes," she said crossly. "I am so hungry right now, I could eat you!"

"Oh, Sara," Ermengarde whispered. "I never knew."

Then her face lit up. "How silly I am!" she said. "My aunt sent me a box today. It is full of good things to eat."

"Oh, Ermengarde!" said Sara. "We can pretend it's a party. Shall we invite the prisoner in the next cell?"

"Oh, yes," said Ermengarde. "The jailer won't hear."

Sara went to the wall. She could hear Becky crying. She knocked four times. "That means: 'Come through the secret passage,'" she told Ermengarde.

Five knocks answered. "That means she's coming!"

Moments later Becky opened the door. But then she saw Ermengarde. One of the young ladies!

"Don't worry, Becky," said Sara. "Ermengarde is bringing us a party."

Ermengarde peeked out the door. The

hall was quiet. She hurried out. In her haste she dropped her red shawl.

"Come, Becky," said Sara. "We must set the table."

"With what, miss?" asked Becky.

Sara spied Ermengarde's red shawl on the floor. "With this fine tablecloth!"

Then Sara found some old handkerchiefs. They became golden plates and fine linen napkins. She took flowers off an old hat. She put them in a cracked mug. "Here's our centerpiece!"

Soon Ermengarde came back and opened her box. The food looked heavenly. Cake. Meat pies. Oranges. Even chocolates!

"It's a queen's table!" Becky said with a sigh.

Then Sara found some scraps of paper. She crumpled them in the fireplace. "It will only burn a minute," she said. "But by then we will forget it's not a real fire."

Sara lit a match. The paper burst into bright, cheery flames.

"Princesses," said Sara. "Be seated."

The girls sat down and began to eat. Yum!

But then they sprang to their feet. Footsteps on the stairs. Someone was coming!

The door banged open. It was Miss Minchin! But she was not alone.

"See, Miss Minchin," Lavinia purred. "I told you."

"Becky," Miss Minchin said. "Go to your room. Now!"

Ermengarde burst into tears. "It's just a party," she whimpered.

"So I see," said Miss Minchin. "With 'Princess Sara' at the head of the table."

She glared at Sara. "Tomorrow you shall have *nothing* to eat!" Then her eyes fell upon the books.

"Ermengarde!" she cried. "Your nice books—here in this dirty attic! I shall write to your father. What if he knew where you are tonight? What would he say?"

Miss Minchin felt Sara watching her. "What is it?" she snapped.

"I was wondering," said Sara. "What if *my* papa saw where *I* am tonight? What would *he* say?"

The candlelight flickered on Sara's face. Miss Minchin shivered.

"How—how dare you!" she managed to say. She swept the food into the box. She picked up the books. Then she shoved Ermengarde out the door.

Sara was alone. The bright fire was in ashes. She picked up Emily and held her tight. "There aren't any princesses," she said. "Only prisoners."

Sara suddenly felt so tired. She crawled into bed. "Suppose there was a nice fire." She yawned. "A hot supper on the table…Suppose…"

Sara was already asleep.

She didn't see the face in the window. But the face saw everything.

18
The Magic

Sara woke up suddenly. It was still dark. At first she didn't open her eyes. She felt so warm. Too warm!

"I must be dreaming," she thought. But an odd sound kept her awake. A crackling sound.

Sara opened her eyes. A fire blazed in the grate. A table was set before the fire. It was crowded with dishes and a teapot. A bright lamp filled the room with soft light. A lamp with a rose-colored shade.

Sara sat up. She rubbed her eyes. There was a pretty satin quilt on her bed.

She swung her feet out of bed. The

floor was covered with a thick blue rug.

It was the room of her dreams.

Sara ran to the fireplace. She held her hands to the fire. "A dream fire would not be so hot," she told Emily.

She ran to the table. Steam rose from the dishes. "Real food!" she cried. "I am not dreaming!"

Then she saw a stack of books. She opened the top one. Someone had written a note. It said: "To the little girl in the attic. From a friend."

Sara ran next door. "Becky!" she cried. She shook her friend. "Come quickly."

Becky was still half asleep. She stumbled behind Sara. Then she saw Sara's room. "Blimey!"

"It's true!" said Sara. "The Magic has been here!"

Becky grabbed a muffin and jammed it into her mouth. "Perhaps we should hurry, miss. In case it melts away."

The food was so good. Hot soup. Sandwiches. Muffins. Tea. They ate until they could not eat another bite.

"This may not be here in the morning," Becky said.

"Yes," said Sara. "But it is here tonight. And I shall never forget it."

The school was abuzz the next morning. Everyone knew what Lavinia had done. Everyone knew Sara Crewe was in disgrace. What would happen to her?

Lavinia was not one bit sorry. "I'm surprised Miss Minchin didn't throw Sara out for good," she said.

Jessie frowned. "Where would she go?"

"How should I know?" said Lavinia. "Who cares?"

Miss Minchin waited for Sara. Sara was too proud. Surely she had broken her this time.

At last Sara came into the classroom. But she did not look broken. Her cheeks were rosy. She was even smiling!

"Sara Crewe!" said Miss Minchin. "Don't you understand? You are in disgrace."

"Yes, Miss Minchin," Sara said.

"Well, then," said Miss Minchin. "Do not forget it. And do not look so smug. You look as if you found a fortune. And remember. You get nothing to eat today."

Sara just smiled. "Yes, Miss Minchin."

"Perhaps she is pretending she had a good breakfast," said Lavinia.

But no one laughed.

The weather was awful that day. Cook was in a terrible mood. Everyone gave Sara more work to do.

But what did it matter? Her supper the night before had given her strength. And Sara had her Magic.

She saw Becky for only a moment that day. But they shared a secret smile.

It was late when Sara's work was done. She almost flew up the stairs.

But she stopped at her door. Her heart fluttered like a caged bird.

"Perhaps it is all gone," she whispered.

Slowly she opened the door. The room *had* changed. But nothing was gone. In fact, the Magic had been there again!

The dirty walls were covered with colorful cloth. Her bed had a new mattress and new pillows.

The fire was blazing once again. And two places were set for supper.

Sara knocked on the wall. Four times: "Come through the secret passage."

The prisoner in the next cell knocked back five times: "I am coming."

In seconds the door slammed open. Becky stood in the doorway.

"Oh, miss!" she cried. "It's still here. Where does it all come from?"

"Let's not even ask," said Sara.

Joyfully they sat down to eat.

The Magic visited every day. Each day some new thing was added. A bookshelf. Fresh flowers. A new chair.

Miss Minchin was as mean as ever. The servants were just as rude. But it did not matter anymore.

"If you only knew!" Sara wanted to shout.

Then one day another Magic thing happened.

The doorbell rang. Sara went to open it. A man held out several packages. They were all addressed the same way: "To the Little Girl in the Right-Hand Attic."

Miss Minchin saw the packages. "Don't just stand there," she told Sara. "Take them upstairs. Who are they for?"

"They are all for me," said Sara.

"What!" Miss Minchin looked at the packages. "Open them at once!"

Sara obeyed. The boxes were full of beautiful clothes. Expensive clothes. A warm new coat.

A note said: "To be worn every day. Will be replaced by others when needed."

Miss Minchin began to pace. She wrung her hands. What was going on? Had she made a mistake after all?

Perhaps Sara had an unknown friend.

An unknown relative. Someone rich. Someone who would not like the way Miss Minchin treated Sara!

"Well," said Miss Minchin nervously. "Someone is very kind to you." She thought a moment. Then she said, "Go put your new clothes on. Then come downstairs. You may have lessons in the schoolroom today. No more errands."

Sara was surprised. When had Miss Minchin spoken so kindly to her? Not since her father died.

A half hour later Sara walked into the schoolroom. She was wearing new clothes.

"Look at Princess Sara!" cried Jessie.

The young ladies stared. For it *was* Princess Sara. She looked as she had once looked. Before she was a servant.

"Perhaps someone left her a fortune," said Jessie.

"Oh, stop it," said Lavinia crossly. "Quit looking at her."

But none of the girls could.

Sara and Becky stayed up late that night. They were warm by the fire. Their stomachs were full. It was hard to say good night.

Then they heard a sound on the roof.

Sara ran to the window. "It's the monkey! Come here," she called. "It's too cold for you out there." The monkey chattered as he jumped into her arms.

Becky laughed. "He's plain-looking, ain't he, miss? What will you do with him?"

"It's too late to take him home," said Sara. "He can sleep here tonight. I will take him home tomorrow."

The monkey curled up on Sara's bed. He slept like a baby at Sara's feet.

19

"It Is the Child!"

The next morning Ram Dass opened the front door. It was Mr. Carmichael. Ram Dass showed him into the sitting room.

"What news?" said Mr. Carrisford. "Did you find her?"

His friend shook his head.

Mr. Carrisford moaned and dropped into his chair.

"Don't worry," said Carmichael. "We shall find her."

The doorbell rang again. Ram Dass went to answer it. It was Sara Crewe. And she had the monkey with her.

Ram Dass led her to the sitting room. "Sir," he said. "It is the little girl from next door."

"Your monkey ran away again," Sara

said. "It was late, and I know you are ill. So I let him stay with me."

"Thank you," said Mr. Carrisford. "That was kind."

Sara handed the monkey to Ram Dass. She spoke to him in his own language.

Mr. Carrisford stared. "How do you know his language?"

"Oh, I was born in India," said Sara.

Mr. Carrisford sat up suddenly. "You were born in India!" He held out his hand. "Come here."

Sara was startled. But she went and stood beside him.

"You live next door?" he asked.

"Yes," she said. "At Miss Minchin's school."

"But you are not a student."

"No." Sara frowned. "I don't know exactly *what* I am."

"Why not?"

"I was a student at first," said Sara. "But now I run errands for Miss Minchin. And I sleep in the attic."

"What do you mean, 'at first'?" Mr. Carrisford asked.

"At first," said Sara. "When my papa took me there."

"Where is your papa now?"

"He died," said Sara. "He lost all his money. There was no one to take care of me. There was no one to pay Miss Minchin. So now I work for her."

Mr. Carrisford choked out the words: "How did your father lose his money?"

"He did not lose it himself," said Sara. "He had a friend. A friend he loved. But the friend took his money and lost it. Papa trusted his friend too much."

"Perhaps it was an accident," Mr. Carrisford whispered. "Perhaps the friend meant no harm."

Sara thought this over. At last she said, "Perhaps. But the pain was still just as bad for Papa. It killed him."

"Tell me..." Mr. Carrisford said. His voice trembled. "What was your father's name?"

"Captain Ralph Crewe," answered Sara. "He died in India."

Mr. Carrisford gasped. "It is the child!" He fell back in his chair. Ram Dass ran to his side.

Sara was frightened. Mr. Carrisford looked so sick. Ram Dass quickly opened a small bottle. He poured drops into a cup and held it to his master's lips.

Mr. Carrisford drank the medicine. He took several deep breaths. He stared at Sara as if she might disappear.

Sara waited till Mr. Carrisford seemed better. Then she asked softly, "What child am I?"

Mr. Carmichael took Sara's hand.

"Mr. Carrisford was your father's friend," he said gently. "The one with the diamond mines. We've been looking for you for two years."

Sara's green eyes grew wide. At first she could not speak. Then she whispered, "And I was just next door."

Sara sat down. Mr. Carmichael

explained everything. At first Mr. Carrisford thought his mines had failed. He thought he had lost all his money. And all of Captain Crewe's money as well. His grief made him ill. He almost died of brain fever.

But then diamonds were found in the mines. Mr. Carrisford wanted to tell Captain Crewe he was rich. But he was too late. Captain Crewe died before he could tell him.

Mr. Carrisford had been searching for Sara ever since.

Ram Dass smiled. "I told Mr. Carrisford about meeting you," he said. "We often saw you pass by our window. We did not know who you were, of course. But he wanted to do something for you—for Sara Crewe's sake. So I slipped into your attic room. I tried to make things nicer for you."

"You brought the Magic?" she cried.

Ram Dass bowed.

She turned to Mr. Carrisford. "And

you sent me all those wonderful things? You were the friend who made the dream come true?"

"Yes, dear child, I did," he said.

He looked so sick. Sara could tell his heart was sick, as well. But there was a kindness in his eyes. It was a look that made her remember her father.

Sara took his hand and kissed it. Mr. Carrisford's face lit up with joy.

The doorbell rang again. Miss Minchin pushed past Ram Dass. She glared at Sara. "So there you are!" she hissed.

She smiled at Mr. Carrisford. A cold, fishy smile. "I do beg your pardon," she said. "This girl is a charity case. I had no idea she was here." She grabbed Sara's arm. "Sara! Go home at once!"

Mr. Carrisford stood up slowly. "She is not going with you. Ever," he said. "Her home is with me now."

Miss Minchin gasped. "But—what does this mean?" she sputtered.

"We have been searching for Sara Crewe," said Mr. Carmichael. Then he explained who Mr. Carrisford was.

"Sara is no longer poor," he added. "She has her fortune back. And of course, the diamond mines."

"D-diamond mines!" stammered Miss Minchin.

"Your 'charity case' is rich," said Mr. Carrisford. "Richer than any princess."

Oh, no! Miss Minchin did not know what to do. She could not lose Sara. Not now that she had all her money!

"She must come home with me," Miss Minchin said. "Captain Crewe left her in my care. She would have starved in the streets if not for me. But I kept her, out of the goodness of my heart.

"Sara dear," she said sweetly. "I have not spoiled you, perhaps. But you know that I have always been fond of you."

Sara's green eyes flashed. "Really, Miss Minchin? I did not know that."

Miss Minchin's face turned red. "Sara!"

she said. "You must do your duty to your papa. Come home with me at once!"

"No," said Sara. "And you know why."

Miss Minchin turned to Mr. Carrisford. "You'll be sorry," she said. "She is not an easy child. She is neither truthful nor grateful."

Ram Dass showed Miss Minchin the door.

The schoolroom was buzzing. Miss Minchin's young ladies knew something was going on.

Ermengarde dashed in. "I have a letter from Sara!" she cried.

"Where is she?" asked Jessie.

"Next door," said Ermengarde. She explained everything. "And guess what? Her diamond mines are *real*. She is rich. And she is *never* coming back. I'm going to see her tomorrow."

Becky heard everything. She was so happy for Miss Sara. But she knew the Magic would soon be gone.

She crept upstairs and peeked in Sara's old room. She just had to have one more look!

A fire was burning. Supper was on the table! Just like all those other nights.

Ram Dass stepped from the shadows. He smiled at Becky's startled face.

"I have a letter for you," he said. "Miss Sara wants you to come see her tomorrow."

His eyes sparkled as if he knew a secret.

20
Sara's Idea

After that everything was different. Sara brought joy to the house next door. Mr. Carrisford got well. Ermengarde and Lottie came to visit often.

The Large Family children came too. Sara was like a child from a story. Only better! They always asked her to tell about the cold, dark attic. About the dream that came true.

Sara was grateful she was no longer cold or hungry. Now she knew what it meant to be rich. Because she knew what it meant to be poor. And Sara would never forget.

One day she had an idea. She told Mr. Carrisford about the hungry child. The one outside the bakery.

"I know there are many hungry children," said Sara. "I want to do something to help them."

Sara told him her idea. Mr. Carrisford smiled. "Wonderful!" he said. "We shall do it first thing tomorrow."

Early the next morning Miss Minchin sat at her desk. She was going over her bills. She was in a bad mood.

She looked out the window. She saw Sara run down the steps next door. Becky ran after her. She was Sara's very own maid now. Both girls looked happy and well fed.

Miss Minchin scowled.

"It serves us right!" said Miss Amelia. "We should have been nicer to her. We should have fed her more."

Miss Minchin whirled around. "Amelia!"

"It's true!" said Miss Amelia. "She saw through us both. She saw that you were mean and hard-hearted. And she saw that I was a weak fool."

Miss Minchin had never seen her sister like this. She stood up and yanked the curtains closed!

Mr. Carrisford's carriage stopped at Mrs. Brown's Bakery. He and Sara went inside.

"Good morning!" Mrs. Brown said cheerfully. Then her eyes grew wide. "I remember you, miss! And yet…"

"You once gave me six buns for fourpence," said Sara.

"Of course!" Mrs. Brown exclaimed. "And you gave five away to a beggar girl! Oh, I could never forget you."

Then she looked Sara up and down. "Excuse me, miss. But you look…well, better than you did that day."

"I am better," said Sara simply. "I am much happier, too. And I've come to ask you to do something for me."

Then she explained her idea. "When you see hungry children, call them in. Give them food. And send the bills to me."

"Why, bless you," said Mrs. Brown. "It will be a pleasure. I cannot afford to do much myself. But I've given away many a bun since that day you came. Just thinking of how wet and cold you were. And yet you gave your food away, as if you were a princess."

"I had to share," said Sara. "The child was even hungrier than I was."

"Ah, yes," said Mrs. Brown. "She has told me about it often."

"Have you seen her?" cried Sara. "Where is she? What happened to her?"

The woman turned toward the back room. "Anne," she called. "Come here, darling."

A smiling child ran into the shop. Sara gasped in delight. It was the hungry little girl! But now she was clean and neat. The wild look was gone from her eyes.

The girl knew Sara at once. She smiled shyly. "Hello, miss."

"I started out giving her odd jobs," Mrs. Brown explained. "She was such a hard little worker! I grew quite fond of her. And so I took her in. She helps me now in the shop, you see. And she is a real joy!"

"Mrs. Brown," Sara said. "Perhaps Anne can give out bread to the children. Since she knows what it is like to be hungry."

"I'd like that, miss!" said Anne.

Then it was time to go. Sara gave Mrs. Brown her address. Mrs. Brown and Anne waved goodbye.

Sara stepped lightly into the carriage. Her face glowed as she told Becky about Anne.

Mr. Carrisford smiled. He knew this was only the beginning of the things Sara Crewe would do. How proud Sara's father would have been.

For never had Sara looked more like a Little Princess than she did right now.

Frances Hodgson Burnett was born in England in 1849. Her family moved to Tennessee in 1865. She began writing stories to help support the family when she was just a teenager. The publication of *Little Lord Fauntleroy* in 1886 brought her fame and fortune. Two years later, *Sara Crewe* was published. It became a best-seller. The author expanded the story. It was published as *A Little Princess* in 1905. *The Secret Garden* (1909) firmly established Ms. Burnett's place in children's literature. She died in Plandome, New York, in 1924.

Cathy East Dubowski always dreamed of having her own magical room in the attic—just like Sara Crewe's. But, alas, she has always lived in apartments or houses whose attics were much too small. Luckily, she can visit Sara's attic room in *A Little Princess* whenever she wants. Ms. Dubowski also has adapted *Black Beauty* and *Peter Pan* in the Stepping Stones series. She lives in Chapel Hill, North Carolina, with her husband, Mark, an illustrator, and their two daughters.

**If you like this story,
try reading these other
Stepping Stone Classics**

The Secret Garden

by Frances Hodgson Burnett
adapted by James Howe

Mary put her hand in her pocket, drew out the key, and found that it fitted the keyhole. She turned the key.

And then she took a deep breath and looked behind her up the long walk to see if anyone was coming. No one was. She held back the swinging curtain of ivy and pushed the door, which opened slowly . . . slowly.

Then she slipped through it, shut it behind her, and stood with her back against it, looking about her and breathing quite fast with excitement and wonder and delight.

She was standing *inside* the secret garden.

Little Women

by Louisa May Alcott
adapted by Monica Kulling

"Jo! Jo! Where are you?" cried Meg. She was calling up into the attic.

"I'm here!" Jo called down.

Meg climbed the narrow stairs. The attic was Jo's favorite spot in the house. Here she could eat apples and read in peace. A pet rat, Scrabble, lived nearby. Scrabble didn't mind Jo's company a bit. Today Jo was wrapped in a quilt.

"I have news!" exclaimed Meg. "Both of us are invited to Mrs. Gardiner's New Year's Eve party. It's tomorrow night! What should we wear?"